Do Your Ears Hang Low?

Hazel Quintanilla

Do your ears hang low?

Do they wobble to and fro?

Can you tie them in a knot?

Can you tie them
in a bow?

Can you throw them over your shoulder...

like a Continental soldier?

Do your ears hang low?

Scan this code for more reading fun!

SRP: $7.99 USD
ISBN 978-1-4867-2402-4
50799 >
9 781486 724024

Flowerpot Press
"Planting the seeds that help young minds grow."
TORONTO • NASHVILLE
www.FlowerpotPress.com
CHC-0708-0586 DS-6004
Made in China/Fabriqué en Chine